P9-CEE-497

The Flute Player

The Flute Player

An Apache Folktale

Retold and Illustrated by Michael Lacapa

Northland Publishing

FIRST EDITION
Second Printing 1991
ISBN 0-87358-500-3

Library of Congress Card Catalog Number 89-63749

Designed by Lisa Brownfield
Manufactured in Hong Kong by Dai Nippon

Lacapa, Michael
The flute player : An Apache folktale /
retold and illustrated by Michael Lacapa.—1st ed.
ISBN 0-87358-500-3 : $14.95
1. Apache Indians—Legends. I. Title
E99.A6L33 1990
398.2'089972—dc20 89-63749
CIP
AC

For all my young Apache friends

who live near and around the canyon.

Also, for Kathy, Daniel, Rochelle,

and Anthony, listeners in the canyon.

Listen!

Did you hear that sound? Some say it's the wind blowing through the trees, but we know it isn't.

A long time ago, down in a valley, there were many people moving in, from far and wide. Every year these people would have a social dance so that the young people could get together.

The women of the village decided when these dances should be held. One evening, the women got together and talked. They decided it was a good time for a hoop dance. So, one was planned.

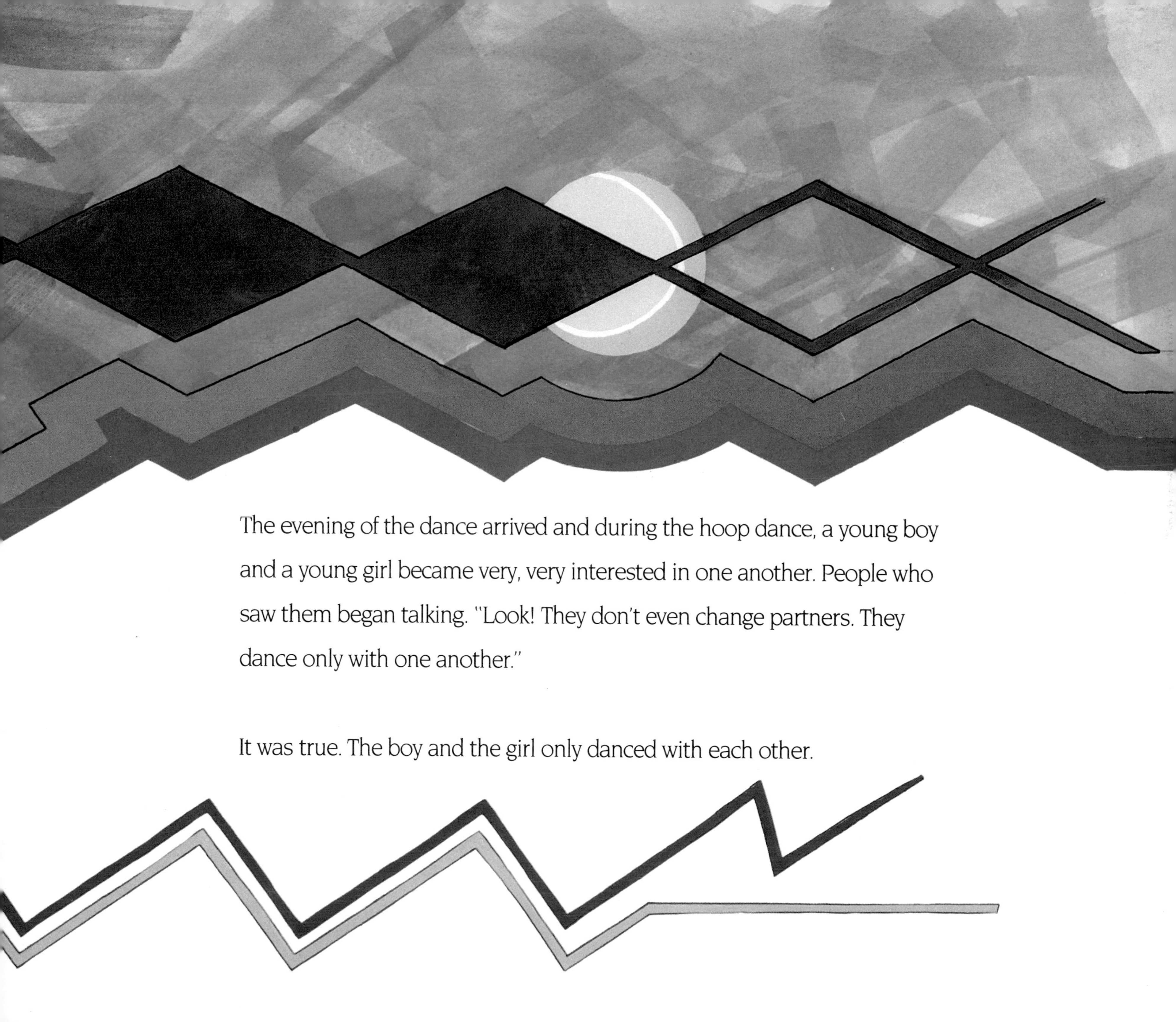

The evening of the dance arrived and during the hoop dance, a young boy and a young girl became very, very interested in one another. People who saw them began talking. "Look! They don't even change partners. They dance only with one another."

It was true. The boy and the girl only danced with each other.

Between the dances,
the boy told the girl,
"I play a flute."

She told him, "Maybe someday, I will hear you play your flute when I go to the canyon to work in my father's field. When I hear you play your flute, I will place a leaf in the river that runs through the canyon. When you see the leaf float past you, you will know that I like your song."

Early the next morning, the boy went to the canyon and played his flute. People working in the canyon in the cornfields said, "Listen, that sounds like the wind blowing through the trees."

The girl listened to the flute player. She liked his song. She pulled a leaf from a tree, took it to the river, and gently dropped it in. She watched it float away.

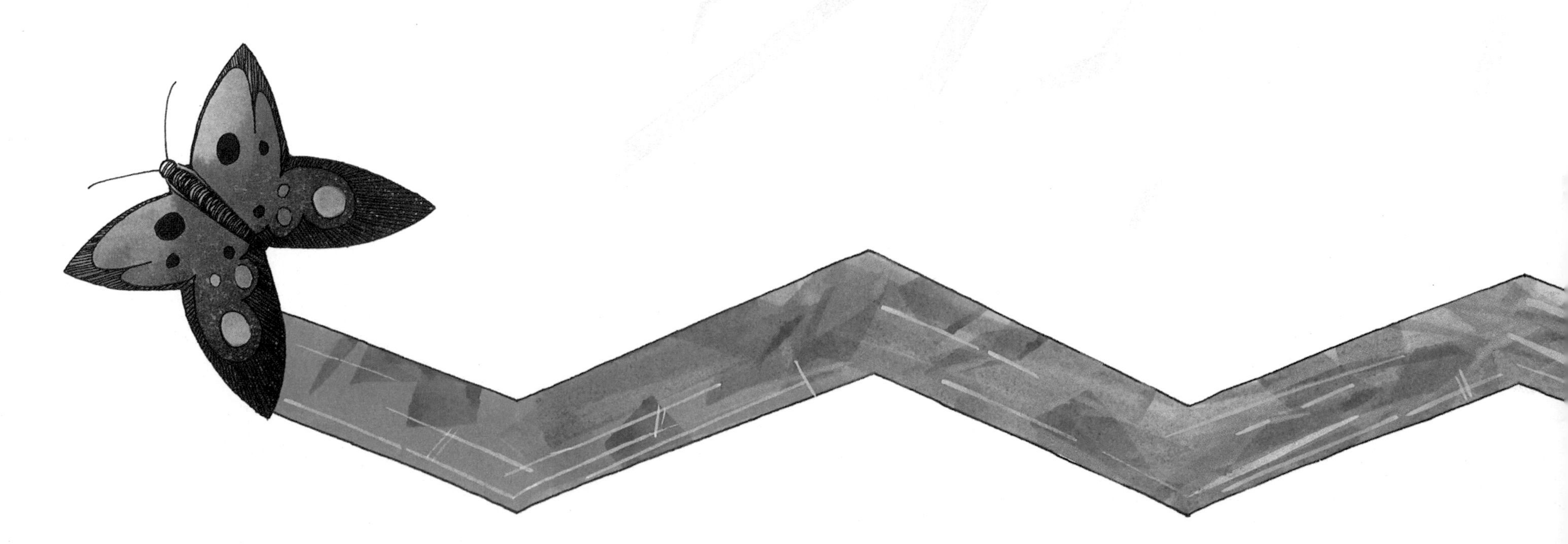

As soon as the boy finished playing his flute, he dashed to the water and looked for the girl's leaf. He saw it, and as it floated by, he picked it up.

He put it in his belt and was very happy. He said to himself, "She likes my playing."

The next day both the boy and girl got up early, and returned to the canyon. The boy played his flute again. The people listened and said, "My, what a beautiful sound. It sounds like the wind blowing through the trees."

The girl heard it, too. Once again, she took a leaf from a tree and placed it in the water.

As soon as he was done playing his song, he went to the river, lifted the leaf from the water, placed it in his belt, and said, "She likes my song. Maybe she likes *me*!"

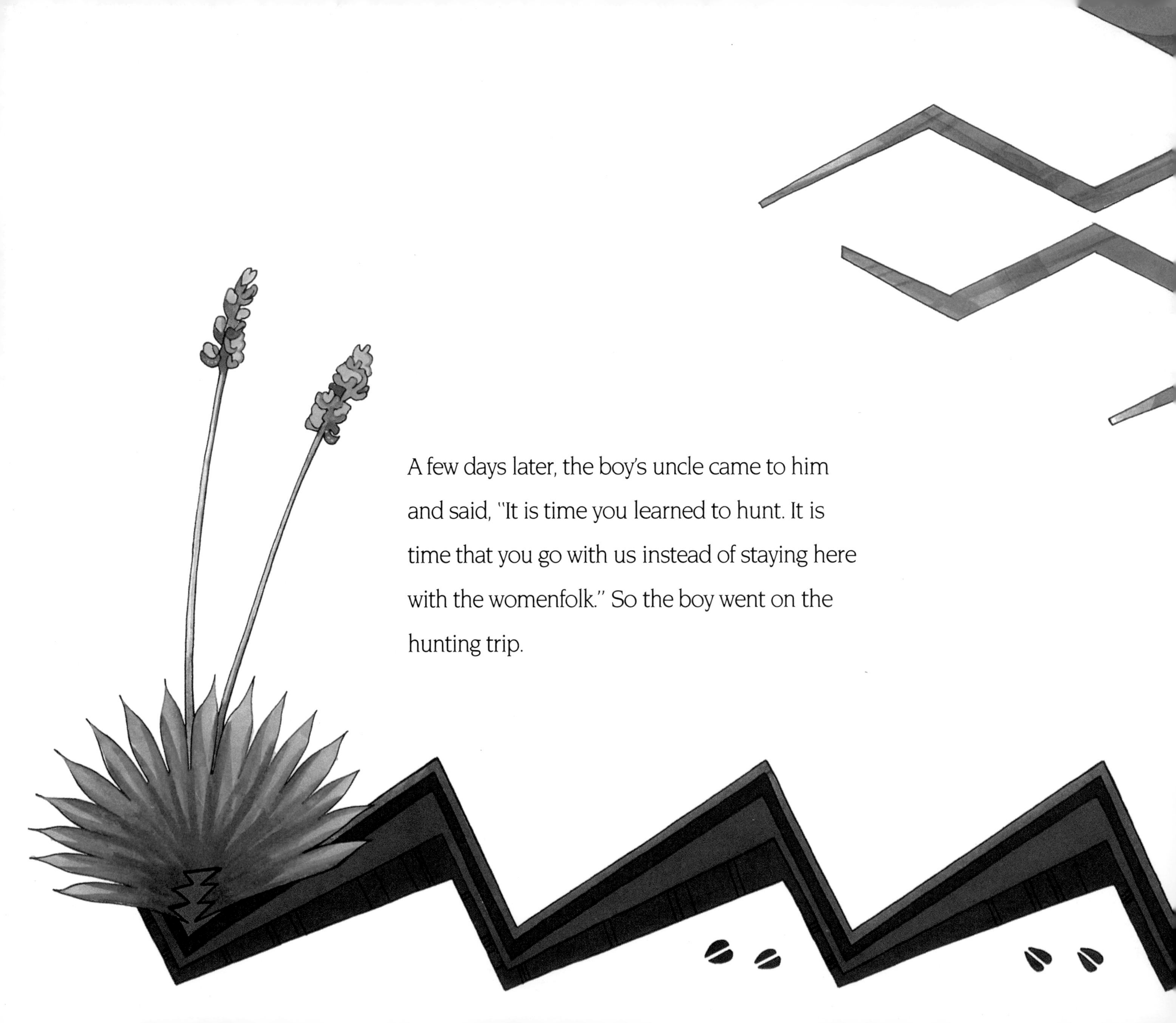

A few days later, the boy's uncle came to him and said, "It is time you learned to hunt. It is time that you go with us instead of staying here with the womenfolk." So the boy went on the hunting trip.

The young girl did not know that he was gone. Early the next morning, she went down to the river and listened for his song. She waited and waited, but she heard nothing.

The next day she got up early, even before the sun was up, she went to the canyon, and waited and listened, listening for his song.

Because the boy was off on the hunting trip, he could not play a song for her, but she did not know this. She thought he didn't like her anymore. This made her sad.

She was so sad that she became very ill. Her family did everything for her. They took her to the medicineman. They said special prayers and gave her special medicine. But she did not get well. Soon, the young girl died.

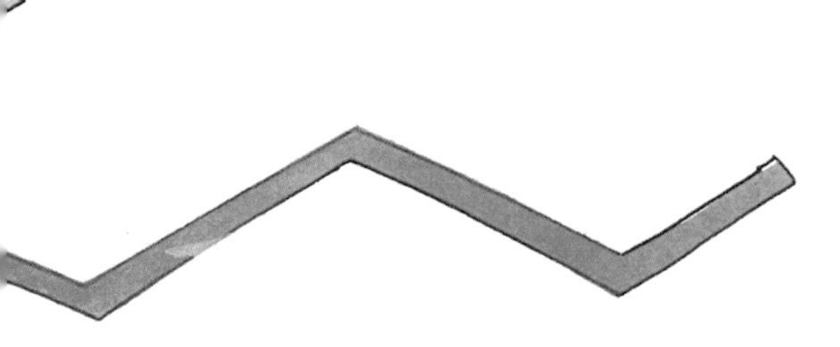

It was a good hunt and there was much game to take to the village. As the boy rode, he played his flute and thought how happy he would be to play for the young girl again.

When the boy got back to the village—before he unloaded his tired horse—he quickly went down to the canyon where the cornfields and the river were. There, he played his flute.

The people looked around and said, "My, listen to that. It's a beautiful sound. It sounds like the wind blowing through the trees."

The boy ran to the river and looked...and saw nothing. He thought maybe it was too late in the day for her to be in the cornfield, and so she did not hear his song. Early the next morning, he went to the canyon where the cornfields were and played his song over and over again. Each time, he ran to the river and watched for her leaf. But he saw nothing.

At the end of the day, the boy was very unhappy. He wondered what had happened, what had he done? Then he saw the girl's brother. He said to him, "Where is your sister?" Her brother looked down. With a sad face, he said that she had gotten sick and died. There had been nothing they could do to make her better.

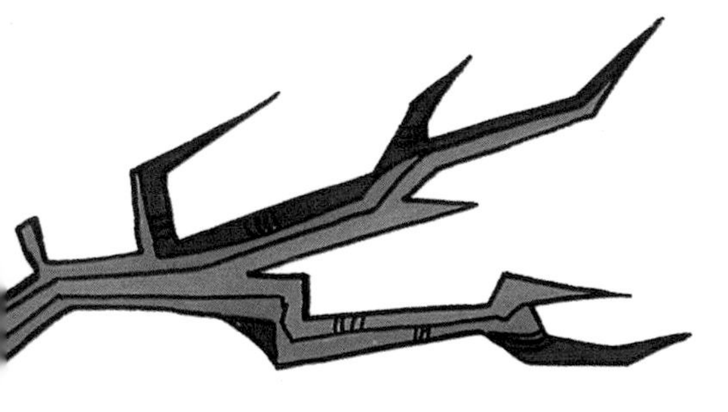

The young boy felt sad. He asked where the family had buried her, and the brother showed him. When the brother left, the boy took out his flute and played a song for her.

Not long after, the boy disappeared. No one knew where he went, and they never saw him again. His family looked and looked for him, but could not find him. They missed him very much.

Today, we go to the canyon, down to the cornfields and the river. We sit and listen to the echoes of the canyon and watch the leaves fall into the river. Some say, "Listen to that beautiful sound. It sounds like the wind, blowing through the trees." But we smile, and know that the girl still likes the flute player.

"Shí goshk'án dasjaá"

(The story ends here.)

I gratefully acknowledge the White Mountain Apache story-tellers I listened to and learned from as I was growing up.

The Apache Language and Culture Program was, at one time, the catalyst for all cultural information for the Tribal Educational Department. All staff members committed themselves to the creation and development of culturally relevant educational materials. I acknowledge my appreciation to Karen Adley, Christina Bead, Bonnie Lewis and Helen Crocker, all former staff members of the Apache Language and Culture Program—although the program no longer exists, we all carry on the spirit.

This is our spirit in print.

MICHAEL LACAPA has been formally trained as a fine artist, with an MFA from Northern Arizona University in Flagstaff. He has worked with the Apache tribe, developing educational materials, and has been "artist-in-residence" at a number of schools state-wide. His stories were learned from elders of the tribes, and he is dedicated to their preservation.